DATE DUE			

The Shadow of a Flying Bird

A Legend from the Kurdistani Jews

Retold and
Illustrated by Mordicai Gerstein

Hyperion Books for Children
New York

AUTHOR'S NOTE

This story is from a Midrash, a text using biblical legends to teach a moral lesson. I found it in Yona Sabar's wonderful book *The Folk Literature of the Kurdistani Jews: An Anthology.* He translated it from a five-hundred-year-old manuscript written in a language called Neo-Aramaic. I am grateful to Professor Sabar for additional information, and to Professor Robert Hoberman, whose translation was also helpful in my retelling.

—M. G.

Text and illustrations © 1994 by Mordicai Gerstein.
All rights reserved.
Printed in the United States of America.
For information address Hyperion Books for Children,
114 Fifth Avenue, New York, New York 10011.

FIRST EDITION
1 3 5 7 9 10 8 6 4 2

Library of Congress Cataloging-in-Publication Data
Gerstein, Mordicai.
The shadow of a flying bird: a legend of the Kurdistani Jews/adapted
and illustrated by Mordicai Gerstein—1st ed.
p. cm.
Summary: Moses, at the end of his life, refuses to give up his
soul to God, who is forced to take it himself with a single kiss.
ISBN 0-7868-0016-X (trade)—ISBN 0-7868-2012-8 (lib. bdg.)
1. Moses (Biblical leader)—Death and burial—Juvenile literature.
[1. Folklore, Jewish. 2. Moses (Biblical leader) 3. Death—Folklore.] I. Title.
BS580.M6G44 1994 296.1'42—dc20 [E] 94-7034 CIP AC

The artwork for each picture is prepared using oil paint on vellum.
This book is set in 14-point Cochin.

For my father, Samuel Gerstein
September 9, 1909 – August 7, 1991

I<small>T IS TOLD THAT WHEN</small> M<small>OSES</small> reached the age of one hundred and twenty, God led him up to the top of Mount Nebo and said, "Look! Before you lies the land of milk and honey. The land that I promised to you and your people."

"At last!" said Moses. "How I've longed to see it."

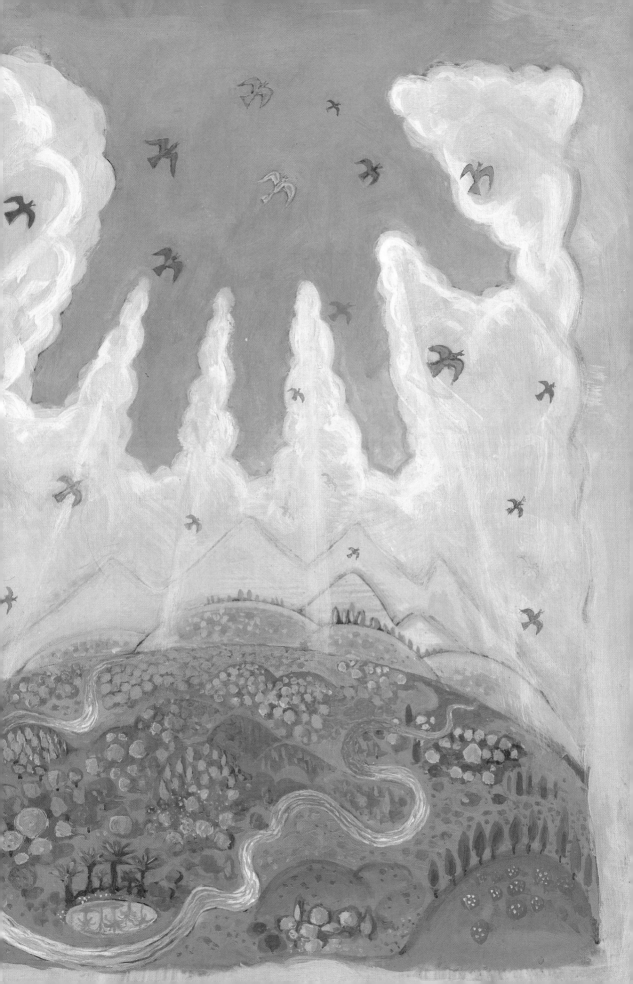

"Look well," said God, "but, sadly, you shall not go there. Your life has reached its end. Now your soul must return to me."

"But Lord," said Moses, "why now? Give me a little longer. My hundred and twenty years seem like one short day."

"A man or woman's life," said God, "is like the shadow of a flying bird. Even if you lived a thousand years, at the end it would seem but one day. Your time has come."

Then Moses stood up and began to pray
that he might live.

Moses prayed five hundred and fifteen
prayers and sent them up to heaven.

"Lock the doors and windows," said God
to His angel Akraziel. "The prayers of Moses
may not enter. His time has come."

"Oh Lord of the World," said Moses, "let me be a fish in the sea. Let me be a sheep that eats grass on the hill. Only let me live."

"Everything born has a time to die," said God. "I cannot change that."

"Dear Lord!" cried Moses. "Turn me into a
tiny butterfly; I'd eat nothing and I'd sleep on
the wind. Just let me live."

"Enough!" said God. "Prepare your soul
for the journey."

Then Moses turned to the hills and
mountains.

"Oh hills and mountains!" he shouted.
"Plead for me. Beg Him to spare me."

And the hills and mountains echoed back,
"Moses, who will plead for us? In time we
too must fall, and the earth itself will
crumble and blow away."

Then Moses raised his voice to the sun
and the moon and the stars.
  "Dear friends, surely He'll listen to you.
Convince Him I must not die!"

And the sun and the moon and the stars replied, "How can we save you when we cannot save ourselves? Don't you know that in time we too must fade and flicker out?"

Then Moses bowed his head.

"Lord of the World," he said, "my soul is
yours. Take it."

And God said
to His angel Gabriel,
"Go down, fetch
the soul of Moses
and bring it home."

"Oh my Lord and King," said Gabriel. "Moses spoke your words to the Pharaoh of Egypt. He parted the sea and led his people to freedom. Who am I to ask him for his soul?"

"You, Michael," said God, "you bring me Moses' soul."

"Oh Lord and Master," said the angel Michael, "Moses led his people through the wilderness. He carved your commandments in precious stone. How can I take his soul?"

God turned to His angel Zagzagle.

"I command you," He said. "Bring me the soul of Moses."

And Zagzagle wept and said, "Oh Lord of Heaven, he is my disciple and I am his teacher. How can I take the soul of one I love?"

Then God turned to Sammael, the envious one, the angel of death, and said, "Fetch me the soul of Moses."

And Sammael grinned and licked his lips. He had waited long for this day.

"Yes, Lord!" he said. "You shall have it right away!"

He took his bitter sword, wrapped himself in a cape of hate, envy, and rage, and he flew down before Moses in a storm of fire.

Moses was writing the secret names of God, and precious gems spilled from his lips and eyes; rainbows streamed from his forehead. Sammael cringed and drew back trembling.

"Evil one!" cried Moses. "My soul won't go with you!" And he picked up his staff and hit Sammael in the eye.

Then Gabriel spread a silken mat for
Moses to lie on, Michael covered him with a
silken sheet, and Zagzagle put a silken pillow
under his head. And God descended to the
top of the mountain and said to the soul of
Moses, "It is time for you to come home
with me."

Half-blind, Sammael fled howling back to heaven and threw himself down before God.

"Please, Lord," he begged. "Ask me to stand heaven on its head. Ask me to blow out the stars, but do not ask me for the soul of Moses."

"Moses," said God, "prepare. I will take your soul myself."

"Dear Lord," said the weeping soul, "how can I leave the body of this man whom I love? Let me stay!"

"Please come," said God. "You shall sit beside me on my throne of glory."

"Oh Lord, forgive me, but I would rather stay with Moses than live in heaven with all the angels."

And when God saw that the soul would not come, He bent over Moses, and with a kiss of His mouth, He took it.

Then God sat down and wept.
"Oh woe! Oh woe! Now who will
oppose evildoers? Who will speak for me
and love me as Moses did? And whom will I
love as well?"

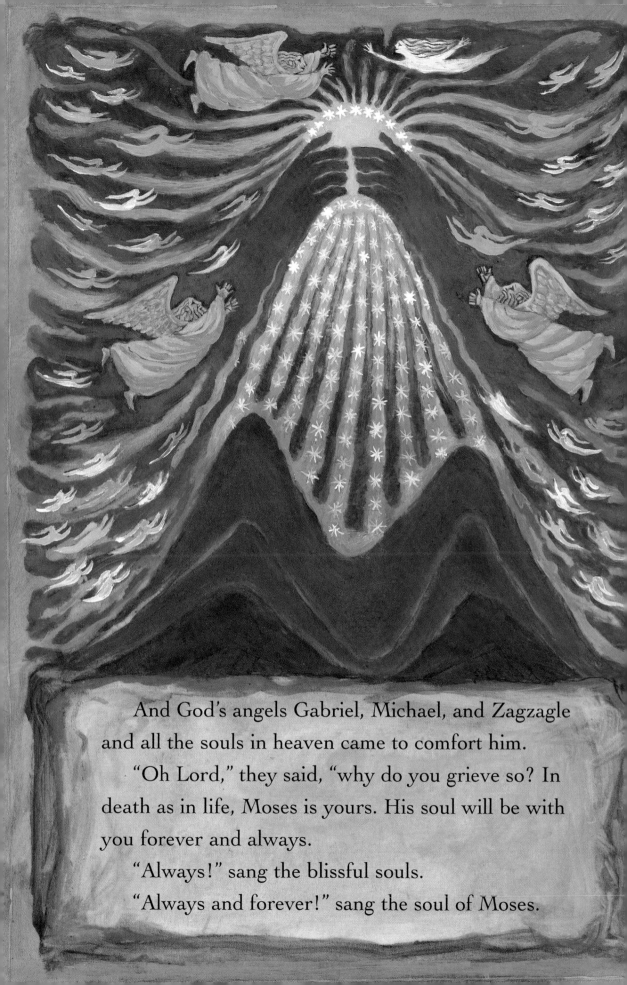

And God's angels Gabriel, Michael, and Zagzagle and all the souls in heaven came to comfort him.

"Oh Lord," they said, "why do you grieve so? In death as in life, Moses is yours. His soul will be with you forever and always.

"Always!" sang the blissful souls.

"Always and forever!" sang the soul of Moses.